```
394.1     Kelley, True
Kel         Let's eat!
```

DATE DUE

NOV 19
NOV 23

MITCHELLVILLE
ELEMENTARY LIBRARY

MITCHELLVILLE
ELEMENTARY LIBRARY

Let's Eat!

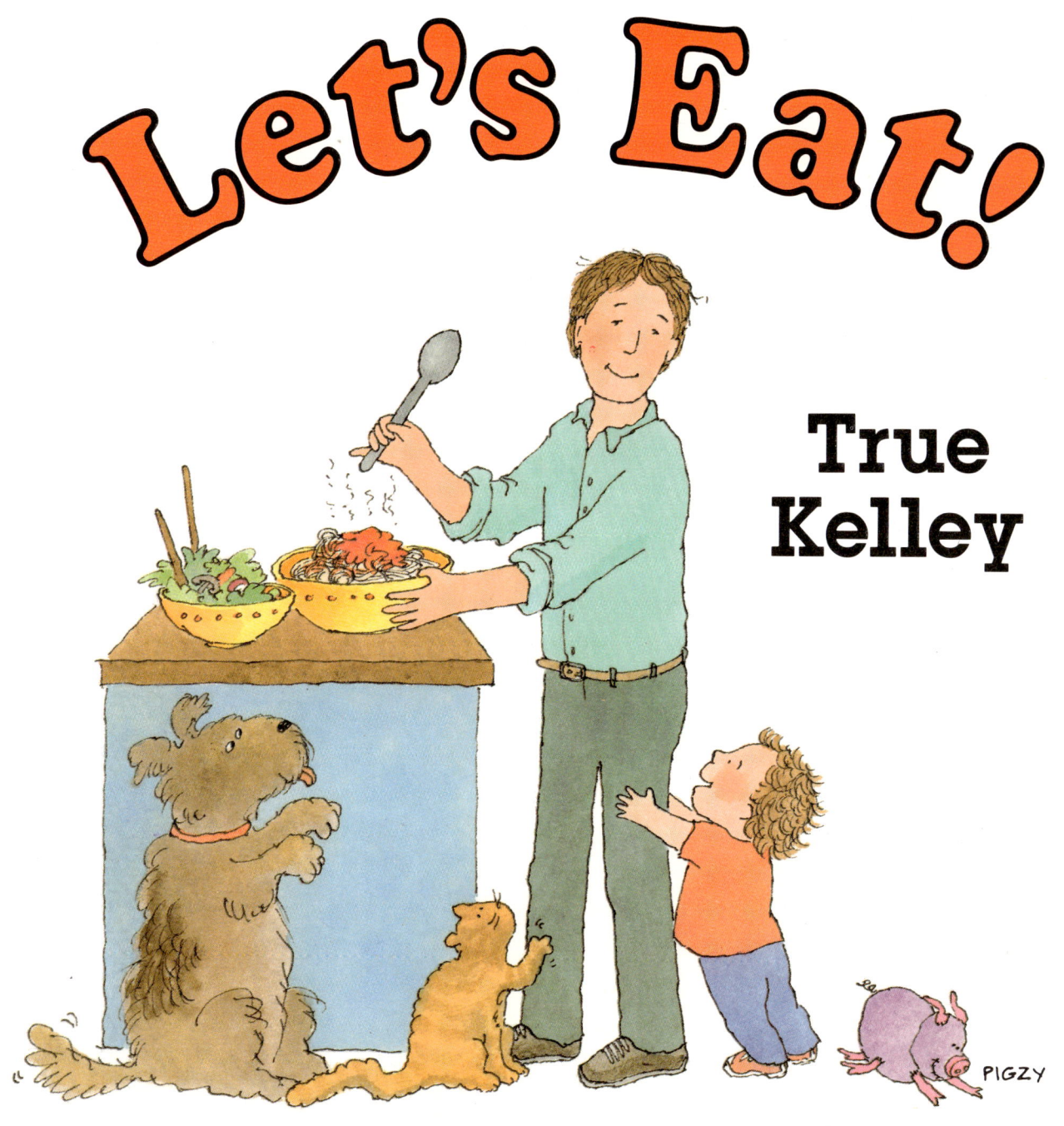

True Kelley

E. P. DUTTON   NEW YORK

Copyright © 1989 by True Kelley
All rights reserved.
Published in the United States by
E. P. Dutton, New York, N.Y.,
a division of NAL Penguin Inc.
Published simultaneously in Canada by
Fitzhenry & Whiteside Limited, Toronto
Designer: Alice Lee Groton
Printed in Portugal
First Edition   10 9 8 7 6 5 4 3 2 1

Library of Congress Cataloging-in-Publication Data
Kelley, True.
  Let's eat!/by True Kelley.—1st ed.
    p. cm.
  Summary: Presents illustrations of where food
comes from, eating places, etiquette, and equipment,
and people eating meals, thinking about food,
and performing food tricks.
  ISBN 0-525-44482-3
  1. Food—Juvenile literature.   2. Dinners and
dining—Juvenile literature.   (1. Food.   2. Dinners
and dining.)   I. Title.   88-25699
TX355.K37   1989   CIP
394.1'2—dc19   AC

for
Eric and Steven Lindblom,
food lovers known for their
feeding frenzies

TASTY!

OINK! OINK!

GNAW TREES OR NIBBLE CHEESE

CRUNCH CRUNCH!

OVER THE TEETH, AND PAST THE GUMS, LOOK OUT, STOMACH, HERE IT COMES!

Favorite Foods

ZOOP!

MUSTARD

GRAND VIEW BLUEBERRY FARM

'LISHUS!

YOU WILL BE

Food comes from...
The Farm

The Sea

Food comes from...
The Garden

The Orchard

Breakfast

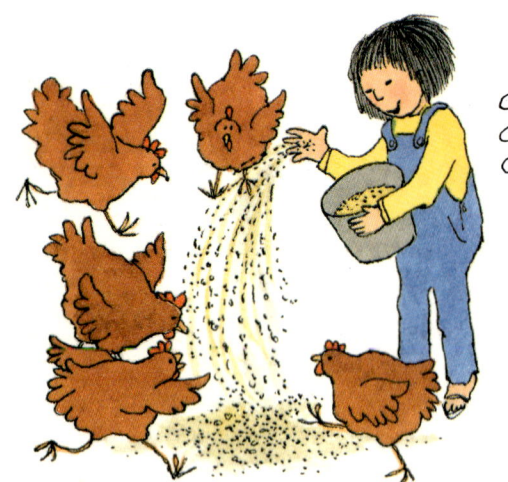

CHICK
CHICK
CHICKEE !

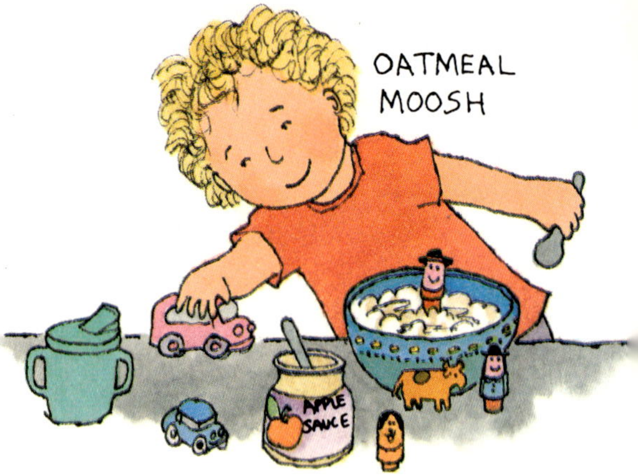
OATMEAL
MOOSH
APPLE
SAUCE

SQUIRT

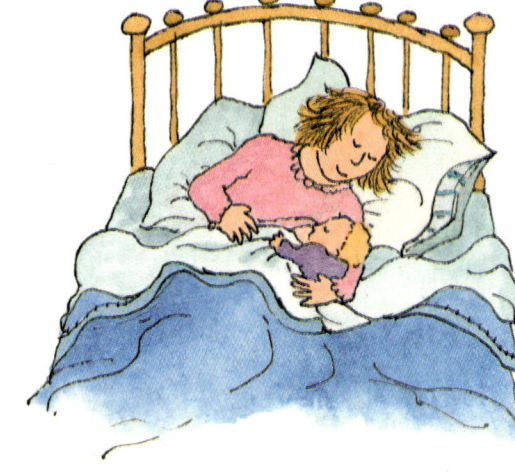

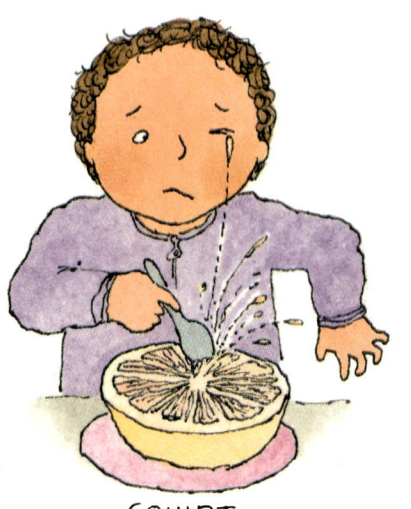

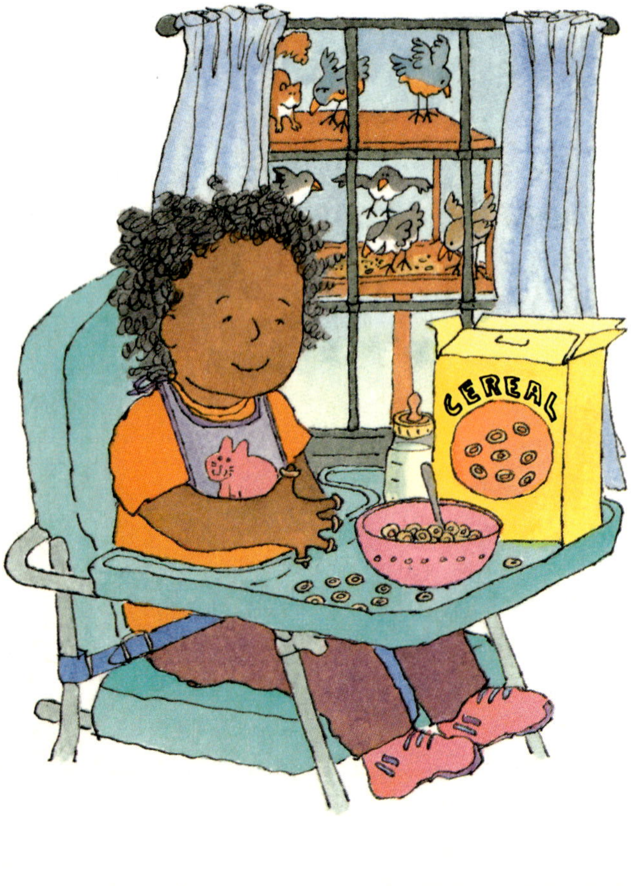
CEREAL

POING
JAM

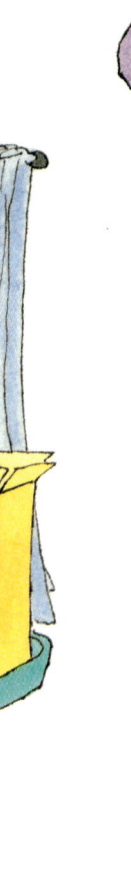

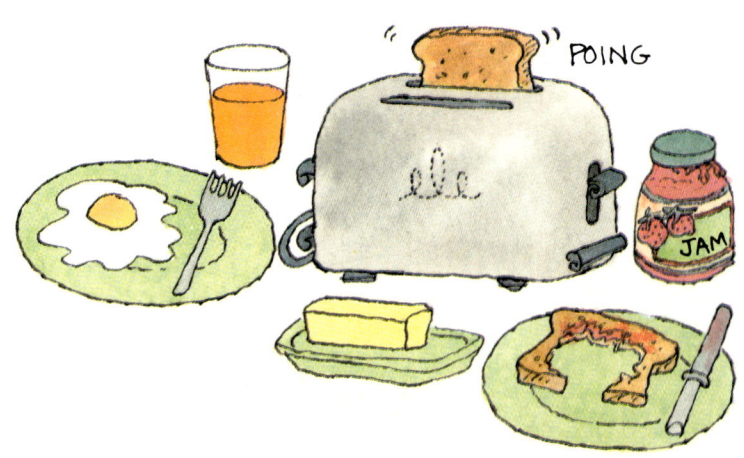

Dinner

SNUFFLE SNUFFLE

TUNA WIGGLE!

STRETCHY CHEESE

WE ARE GRATEFUL FOR THE EARTH'S GIFTS.

Snack

SNEAKY SNACKY

EARLY BIRD SPECIAL

YOGURT

SCALLIONS ?!

A Kitchen

Eating Equipment

TEETH!

Eating Everywhere...

FLYING FOOD